for Marsha Dixon

Text copyright © 1994 by Ruth Brown
All rights reserved.

CIP Data is available.

First published in the United States 1994 by
Dutton Children's Books,
a division of Penguin Books USA Inc.
375 Hudson Street, New York, New York 10014
Originally published in Great Britain 1994 by
Andersen Press Ltd., London.
Typography by Carolyn Boschi
Printed in Italy
First American Edition
1 3 5 7 9 10 8 6 4 2
ISBN 0-525-45326-1

COPYCAT

∽ RUTH BROWN ∽

Dutton Children's Books ∽ New York

This is a story about four friends who live together: Bessie the dog, Holly the cat, and Holly's two children, Baby and Buddy. Holly is a lazy cat and likes to lie around all the time. Baby is shy and keeps to herself. But Buddy is a copycat. Can you guess which one he is?

Holly likes to daydream by the window. So does Buddy.

So does Buddy.

When the humans are not home,
Bessie likes to lie on the couch.
Buddy lies down, too.

Buddy copies the squirrels
on the garden wall

the birds.

He even tries to chew
on Bessie's bone!

Poor copycat.

Cats' teeth aren't made
for chewing bones.

Buddy has three broken teeth.
He has to go to the vet.
Nobody wants to copy Buddy!

Now Buddy feels better. His tongue hangs out a little, but he hasn't changed one bit.

He's still the
same old copycat.